Mr. Gumpy's Outing

John Burningham

Henry Holt and Company · New York

EASY
BUR

July
2000

Library of Congress Catalog Card Number: 77-159507
ISBN: 0-8050-0708-3 (hardcover)
20 19 18 17 16 15 14
ISBN: 0-8050-1315-6 (paperback)
10 9 8 7

Typography and title page design by Jan Pienkowski
First Owlet edition 1990
Printed in Mexico

This is Mr.Gumpy.

Mr. Gumpy owned a boat and his house
was by a river.

One day Mr. Gumpy went out in his boat.

"May we come with you?" said the children.

"Yes," said Mr. Gumpy,
"if you don't squabble."

"Can I come along, Mr. Gumpy?"
said the rabbit.

"Yes, but don't hop about."

"I'd like a ride," said the cat.

"Very well," said Mr.Gumpy.
"But you're not to chase the rabbit."

"Will you take me with you?" said the dog.

"Yes," said Mr.Gumpy.
"But don't tease the cat."

"May I come, please, Mr. Gumpy?"
said the pig.

"Very well, but don't muck about."

"Have you a place for me?" said the sheep.

"Yes, but don't keep bleating."

"Can we come too?" said the chickens.

"Yes, but don't flap," said Mr. Gumpy.

"Can you make room for me?" said the calf.

"Yes, if you don't trample about."

"May I join you, Mr. Gumpy?" said the goat.

"Very well, but don't kick."

For a little while they all went along happily but then...

The goat kicked

The calf trampled

The chickens flapped

The sheep bleated

The pig mucked about

The dog teased the cat

The cat chased the rabbit

The rabbit hopped

The children squabbled

The boat tipped ...

and into the water they fell.

Then Mr. Gumpy and the goat and the calf
and the chickens and the sheep and the pig
and the dog and the cat and the rabbit and
the children all swam to the bank and climbed
out to dry in the hot sun.

"We'll walk home across the fields,"
said Mr. Gumpy. "It's time for tea."

"Goodbye," said Mr. Gumpy.
"Come for a ride another day."